THE MAGICAL UNICORN SOCIETY
UNICORNS, MYTHS AND MONSTERS

Michael O'Mara Books Limited

With special thanks to Anne Marie Ryan

Edited by Jonny Leighton
Designed by Claire Cater and Jack Clucas
Cover design by Angie Allison

Interior illustrations by Kristina Kister and Olga Baumert
Cover illustrations by Kristina Kister

First published in Great Britain in 2021 by Michael O'Mara Books
Limited, 9 Lion Yard, Tremadoc Road, London SW4 7NQ

W www.mombooks.com
f Michael O'Mara Books
🐦 @OMaraBooks
📷 @omarabooks

A CIP catalogue record for this book is available from the British Library.

ISBN: 978-1-78929-349-4

2 4 6 8 10 9 7 5 3 1

Printed in China

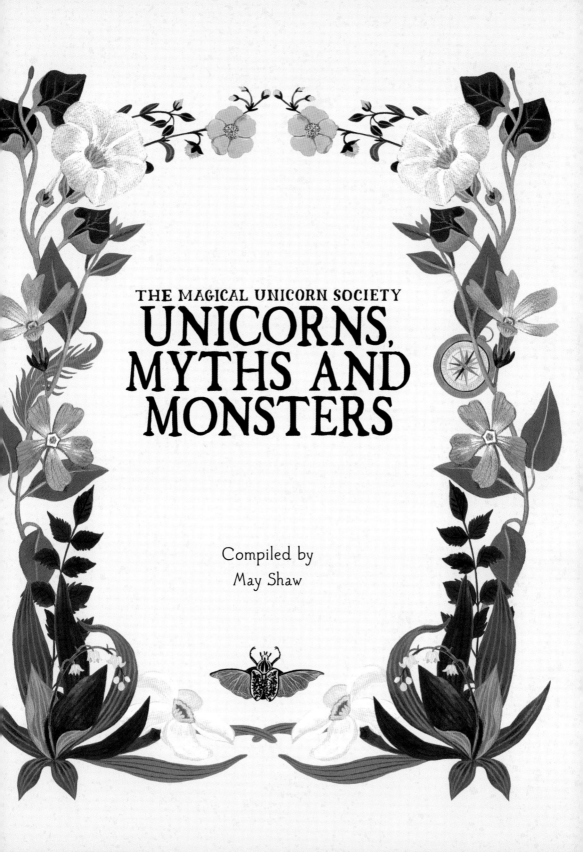

THE MAGICAL UNICORN SOCIETY

UNICORNS, MYTHS AND MONSTERS

Compiled by
May Shaw

CONTENTS

WELCOME

Greetings friends,

My name is May Shaw, and I'm the head of the Magical Unicorn Society's Department of Unicorns, Myths and Monsters.

The Magical Unicorn Society exists to protect and preserve the magic of unicorns wherever they're found, and to tell their amazing stories far and wide. It is our mission to inspire people with tales of their enchanting abilities and adventures.

From our headquarters in London, our researchers, explorers, writers and adventurers set out across the globe to track down members of the eight special families of unicorn. They seek to learn more about them and to fill the Society's vast library with knowledge about these amazing beings.

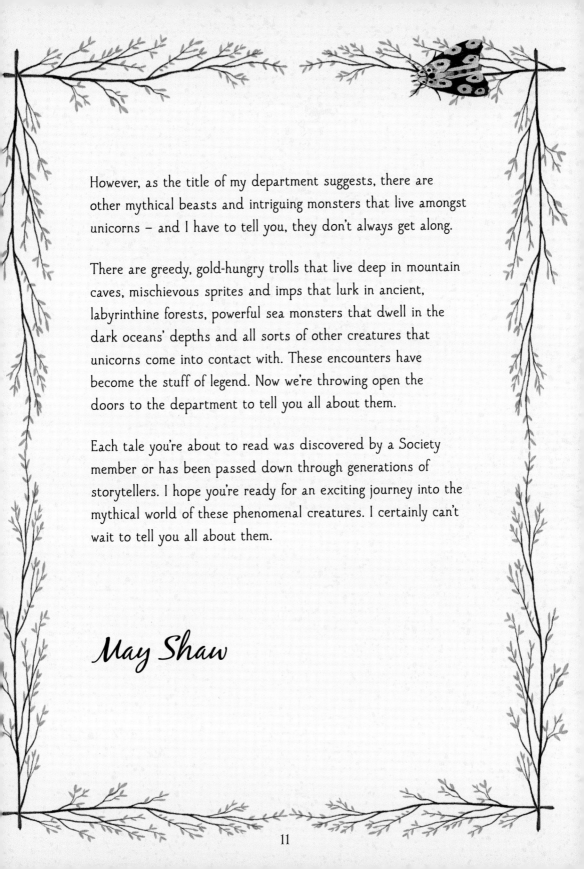

However, as the title of my department suggests, there are other mythical beasts and intriguing monsters that live amongst unicorns – and I have to tell you, they don't always get along.

There are greedy, gold-hungry trolls that live deep in mountain caves, mischievous sprites and imps that lurk in ancient, labyrinthine forests, powerful sea monsters that dwell in the dark oceans' depths and all sorts of other creatures that unicorns come into contact with. These encounters have become the stuff of legend. Now we're throwing open the doors to the department to tell you all about them.

Each tale you're about to read was discovered by a Society member or has been passed down through generations of storytellers. I hope you're ready for an exciting journey into the mythical world of these phenomenal creatures. I certainly can't wait to tell you all about them.

May Shaw

Unicorns, myths, monsters and more,

Are waiting for you, through this door.

THE UNICORN FAMILIES

There are eight enchanting unicorn families that appear in this book.
They each have their own magical abilities and unique appearances.

WATER MOONS

These unicorns are blessed with
the ability to walk on water, and they
help sailors when they're in need.

SHADOW NIGHTS

Shadow Nights often appear in dreams
or at times of great distress. They
have horns made of precious onyx.

WOODLAND FLOWERS

Roses and lilies are woven into the
manes and tails of these unicorns.
They also have special healing magic.

ICE WANDERERS

Ice Wanderers have white coats
that sparkle with magic. They can
communicate over vast distances.

STORM CHASERS

With power over the elements and manes and tails that crackle with electricity, these are powerful unicorns.

MOUNTAIN JEWELS

Tough, hardy and loyal, Mountain Jewels are the strongest and sturdiest of all the unicorn families.

DESERT FLAMES

Desert Flames are some of the fastest unicorns of all. When they reach certain speeds, they can also fly!

DAWN SPIRITS

These beautiful unicorns only appear early in the morning. They can grant wishes to those in need.

We also know of the Golden Unicorn and the Silver Unicorn. These two creatures were the first ever unicorns in existence, and the most powerful of them all. The Silver Unicorn features in the first story.

Apep the Serpent

Apep is an Ancient Egyptian deity embodied by a fearsome, giant snake. It is the bringer of chaos and darkness.

Eyes with hypnotic powers

Jewelled body which gives it super strength

Strong, whipping tail

MYTH FILE ONE:

Eyes of Doom

Apep the Serpent has long been
known to scholars of Ancient Egypt.
Stories tell of his frequent battles
against Ra the Sun God. Apep uses
his hypnotic powers to distract
his enemies, and his strong,
coiling body to crush them.

But Apep has also had encounters
with the Silver Unicorn - one of the
first, and most powerful, unicorns to
ever come into existence. The following
story was discovered on an ancient
papyrus scroll by an M.U.S. explorer.

The Silver Unicorn
and the Snake

Apep the Serpent coiled his slithering, glittering body around and around, rising up to tower over the terrified man and woman that huddled in the shadows of the cave.

"Even the gods cannot contain me," the giant serpent hissed.
"You are mere peasants who live by the banks of the Nile!
You *will* bow to my might."

He swayed forward and looked right into their eyes. His own,
dark pupils swirled with a potent dark magic, transfixing them
both. Powerless to resist him, powerless to run, they were
powerless to save themselves.

"Yes," Apep hissed. "Give in. You won't suffer ... for long."

The man and the woman knelt on the dusty ground and bowed
their heads. The power of the snake monster's hypnotic glare
had made them his willing servants, ready to do his bidding.

〜

Meanwhile, in a magnificent palace that stood on the banks of
the Nile, a young servant girl was busy making cakes for a lavish
banquet, when she was interrupted by a gruff voice barking
orders.

"You girl! Come with me."

Chione jumped. The palace steward, who wore a crisp white kilt,
was standing at the entrance to the kitchen, pointing right at her.

"Me?" Chione asked.

"Yes you," the steward said. "Get a move on. We haven't got all day."

Chione quickly did as she was told and followed the steward out of the kitchen.

"What's this about?" Chione asked, playing nervously with the silver unicorn charm she wore around her neck.

"One of the queen's maids and a kitchen porter didn't turn up for their duties this morning," the steward huffed, shaking his bald head and sighing. "Those ungrateful peasants don't seem to want to serve her majesty - it's the third time this week that servants have not shown up without word or warning."

The steward handed Chione a delicate fan made of ostrich feathers and they rounded a corner, stopping at a set of heavy wooden doors.

"Just keep quiet and do your job, OK?"

Chione nodded.

With a little ceremony, servants on either side heaved at the brass handles, opening the doors to the throne room within.

"Wow," Chione gasped.

Queen Cleopatra's opulent hall stretched out in front of her. The woman herself, reclining on a throne carved with intricate unicorns, looked god-like. Her long, black hair glistened with scented oils and her forearms sparkled with gold bracelets. Chione dashed across the room to take her place opposite another maid and began to move the delicate fan slowly up and down. The queen remained deep in conversation with an adviser who knelt at her feet.

"Still there is no harvest. People are afraid to till the land." Cleopatra said. "How *will* I feed my empire?"

The adviser trembled, fearful of displeasing the queen.

"Your majesty," he mumbled. "They say—"

"What?" she interrupted.

The adviser summoned his courage.

"They say that one of the old monsters has returned. A snake by the name of Apep."

Cleopatra considered this for a moment.

"Go on ..."

Apep the snake monster was once the enemy of kings and queens of Egypt, the adviser explained. A fearsome creature, his body thicker than an ox, fangs as long as a scythe, he was created by the gods as a kind of pet. But soon he grew so hungry for his own power that he shook the very foundations of Egypt. His victims were the people of the Nile - farmers, boatmen, villagers. He was able to hypnotize them, turning them into living dolls he could control in any way he wanted.

"And what happened?" Cleopatra asked.

"He was banished, your Highness," the steward said. "By the power of the Silver Unicorn. Except now - and with so many people missing - he's believed to have returned."

Chione's ears pricked up. Her hand went straight to the amulet around her neck. She couldn't help but think the worst about the maid and the kitchen porter who hadn't turned up that day.

"And this 'Silver Unicorn'?" Cleopatra asked. "Another one of the gods' pets?"

"No!" the steward cried, finding his voice. "It is a being of pure

good that can be summoned only by a tiny few of the Nile's favoured daughters."

Cleopatra pondered for a moment.

"Then I trust something will be done!"

Later, Chione walked home from the palace, back to her family's humble dwelling by the water. She couldn't shake the words of the queen's adviser. The Silver Unicorn could be summoned by a tiny few. By a 'Nile daughter'. Wasn't that what her grandmother had said when she'd given her the amulet? Who, if not she, was a daughter of the Nile? Perhaps it was her duty - in the face of this evil - to do something.

The river mud beneath her bare feet squelched as she followed the edge of the bank. Suddenly, her leg gave way beneath her and she stumbled. Picking herself up and brushing off the clumps of mud that had stuck to her tunic, she noticed something.

"A track," she said.

Then, looking more closely, she saw that the deep, meandering grooves could only be that of a snake - a big one, at that.

Fear raged inside Chione, but the riverbanks were her home, and Egypt was imperilled. She needed to know if Apep really was stalking the banks of the river, and this could be a clue.

She made up her mind and quietly followed the trail away from the riverbank until she came to the entrance of a cave. Pushing aside the reeds that lined its entrance, she stepped inside, and immediately realized she was in trouble. The ground beneath her feet crunched. She was standing on jewelled scales that she could only assume came from the dreaded serpent.

"Uh oh," she gasped.

Sure enough, a low hiss came from the back of the cave, followed by a rustling noise as something immense slithered forward. Chione recoiled as she saw a hideous creature whose gaping mouth was darker than the midnight sky, and whose two piercing eyes bore into her own. Its jewelled body, flowing like the Nile, rippled with terrifying strength.

"Who dares disturb Apep?" the snake hissed angrily.

Chione swallowed her fear and held fast.

"I. Chione. Nile daughter."

Rattling his tail menacingly, Apep slithered closer still, his eyes scorching with hypnotizing power. Chione glanced into the back of the cave. The missing maid and the kitchen porter from the palace were kneeling there, transfixed and still. Apep swooped back into her field of vision, fixing her to the spot with his gaze.

"Stay still, Nile daughter," Apep hissed.

Chione fought the pull of the hypnotizing eyes. It felt like a raging current dragging her out to sea. The only thing to cut through the fog of her thoughts were the welcome words of her grandmother.

The Silver Unicorn!

Chione's fingers grasped the amulet around her neck. It was so hot it burned her hand, shocking her out of her trance. It gave her just enough time to dash out of the cave, before Apep struck.

"Not today, serpent!" she cried.

Chione ran, bursting out into the night. Suddenly, up ahead, a magnificent creature appeared, silhouetted against the full moon. Its crystal horn glittered in a shaft of moonlight and its silver mane flickered in the breeze. In one swift motion, just ahead of Chione, it reared up on its back legs and smashed its hooves into the ground.

A shockwave coursed across the earth. Chione dived for cover among the reeds and Apep the serpent shuddered, caught off guard.

"Yes!" she cried. The Silver Unicorn *had* come to her aid when she'd needed it, just like her grandmother said.

But there was no time to sit back and relax. Apep and the Silver Unicorn were squaring up to fight. Apep's forked tongue flicked from side to side in fury and his body coiled, ready to strike. Nostrils flaring, the unicorn reared again, waving its front hooves in the air.

Apep sprang forward, fangs bared. He caught the unicorn's flank, causing it to let out a whinny of pain.

"Stay away, creature," Apep spat. "This is my land."

The unicorn dodged Apep's writhing body, but the ground was wet and thick with mud. Soon its hooves were bogged down and Apep was gaining the upper hand. Chione cried out as the snake wrapped itself around the unicorn's body.

"No!" Chione shouted.

Quickly she scoured the ground and found a rock. It felt weighty in her palm - enough to cause some damage. She yelled at Apep. When he swung in her direction, she flung the rock square at the snake monster's face.

"This is for the daughters of the Nile!" she yelled.

Apep screeched as the rock smashed against the side of his head. The Silver Unicorn used the moment to wriggle free and rear up on its hind legs. This time, when they came down, a dazzling flash of magical light filled the sky.

Chione shielded her eyes from the blinding glare.

There was a loud hiss and the smell of smoke filled the air. Chione lowered her hands and saw the serpent writhing in agony. As she watched, the snake shrank smaller and smaller, shedding his jewelled skin like a husk, until Apep was just a defeated, pink worm.

The unicorn kicked Apep - and all that remained of him - into the crack in the ground, casting him back to the underworld from where he came.

"Thank you," Chione whispered, stroking the unicorn's silky silver mane. The unicorn lowered its head, touching its horn to Chione's necklace charm as if in blessing. Then, it turned and galloped towards the river, its long tail swishing as it vanished across the water.

Rain began to fall, soaking the soil and swelling the river. The kitchen porter and palace maid stumbled out of the snake's lair in a daze, confused and as if waking from a long sleep. Chione closed her eyes and lifted her face, letting the cool raindrops stream down her cheeks. She couldn't wait to tell the queen that Egypt was safe from the snake monster once more.

Sand Dragon

Sand Dragons patrol their territories in the canyons of American deserts. Their flames burn with a terrible magic.

Flames with the power of dark magic

Thick, scaly skin for defence

MYTH FILE TWO:

Strange Flames

Sand Dragons have lived in cliff caves
and canyon bluffs for eons. They are solitary
creatures that fiercely guard their territory.
They can fly swiftly and their flames have
the power to strip other magical creatures
of their supernatural abilities.

But Desert Flame unicorns, with their bronze
horns and super speed, are a match for any
dragon. The following story, passed down
through generations of people who live near
the Scorched Canyon, shows just that.

*Strong wings
for super speed*

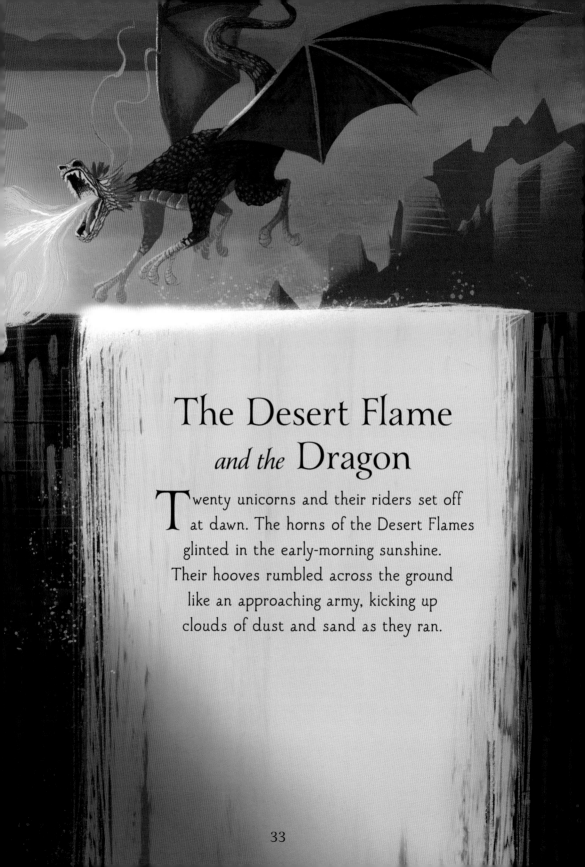

The Desert Flame
and the Dragon

Twenty unicorns and their riders set off
at dawn. The horns of the Desert Flames
glinted in the early-morning sunshine.
Their hooves rumbled across the ground
like an approaching army, kicking up
clouds of dust and sand as they ran.

"Let's go, Blaze!" I cried into my Desert Flame's ear, encouraging her onwards.

Blaze made a strong start, the hills along our homeland becoming a blur of red, pink and purple as we streaked past them. I had to grip on tight as she thundered across the wide open plain.

We galloped towards Scorched Canyon - a dangerous and wild land that was part of the course we had to take to complete the race that had been run for centuries. Unicorn and rider working as one, competing for victory, pride and honour. I was wild, young and a fierce rider, but it was my best friend and rival, Tasha, who had taken the lead on her own impressive Desert Flame, Wildfire.

"You should try flying, Marin," she called over her shoulder teasingly. "Then maybe you'd have a chance against us."

"I don't need to fly to beat you," I called back. "Just you see ..."

Desert Flame unicorns have the power of flight, but they only use it in exceptional circumstances. As important as the race was, this wasn't one of those times. Becoming Desert Champion - the fastest unicorn and rider on the Western plains - requires more than just speed. The winners need endurance and cunning. Months of training had made Blaze and I fitter than any other team. And as for speed, I had a plan ...

Most racers took the high path along the cliffs of the canyon - a safer route, away from the danger that was said to lurk below. But I was fearless, brave, and maybe a little reckless. I decided to take the hard way, a shorter path along the floor of the canyon. It would lead us to victory.

I shifted my weight and Blaze responded at once. She veered off from the pack of racers and headed straight down towards the canyon's sloping sides.

"What are you doing?" shouted Tasha. "You idiot ... you know the stories of the things that lurk down there."

"I'm winning the race, that's what I'm doing," I called back. "And as for what's down there, nothing is a match for racers like me and Blaze."

I dug my heels into Blaze's flanks and we galloped on, leaving Tasha and Wildfire in a cloud of dust. When we arrived at the canyon's edge, Blaze faltered, reluctant to descend and fearful of the steep drop below. But I coaxed her over and she gingerly moved down the slope, pebbles and rocks trickling down the slope ahead of her.

"That's it," I soothed. "Nearly there."

If only I had paid attention to my unicorn's unease, the way she responded to my commands.

When we made it safely to the bottom at last, Blaze was still acting skittish, which wasn't like her at all. Her ears twitched at the slightest sound. At one moment a jackrabbit darted across our path and she reared up, nearly throwing me off her back.

"Settle down," I said as gently as I could. "Nothing can stop us from winning now."

How wrong I was.

Quicker than the jackrabbit, a dark shadow flashed across the canyon. Blaze whinnied and reared up again, waving her hooves in the air, nose flaring. I squinted up at the huge shape blocking out the Sun. At first, I thought it was a bird, but as the creature flew closer, I saw no feathers, just rippling scales covering wings the size of a ship's sail. A leathery crest surrounded the creature's head like a hood and horns ran down its back to the tip of its spiked tail.

This was no bird. It was a terrifying monster from the elders' stories and it was bearing down on us, fast.

"A Sand Dragon," I cried. "Gallop, Blaze. Quickly!"

My heart thumped in time to Blaze's frantic hooves as she quickened her pace. But it was clear that one of the legendary dragons had spotted us. It let out a piercing cry that echoed across the canyon as it swooped down to block our path. Clouds of stinking smoke rose from its nostrils. It bared its teeth in anger. Sand dragons were fierce protectors of their territory. This one did NOT want visitors.

I had led my unicorn and I into a dangerous place and I felt sick to my stomach. I felt like giving up and accepting my fate, but Blaze had other ideas.

The Desert Flame took a step forward and with an elegant jump, took flight into the dust-dry air. With ripples of magic that streamed off her body, we flew up and above the dragon, which was left snapping at our heels.

"Yes, Blaze!" I cried.

Roaring furiously, the Sand Dragon gave chase and came close enough to slash at us with its razor-sharp claws. The dragon was ten times her size, but Blaze was fast and nimble. We ducked and dived, avoiding the dragon's blows. We had nearly made it out of the canyon, when the Sand Dragon lashed at us with its tail, catching one of Blaze's hind legs and whipping us through the air so fast I nearly fell off her back.

I thought we were doomed, but Blaze turned and kicked out with her front legs, hitting the dragon's scaled belly with a loud THUD.

"Attagirl!" I hollered.

But the fight wasn't over yet. The dragon flew at us again, its black eyes smouldering like lumps of coal. Smoke billowed from its nostrils as it spewed a jet of acid green flame. We swerved to avoid it, but a fireball hit Blaze's tail.

Struck by the magical fire, Blaze and her own magic faltered. Her legs flailed and we started to fall. Blaze's magic was strong, but it couldn't withstand the Sand Dragon's flame.

"Fly!" I cried, desperately. But Blaze began plummeting towards the earth. We tumbled down, landing in a river with a splash.

Spluttering, I clung to Blaze's mane as the raging rapids swept us downstream. We would have been submerged if I hadn't managed to grab onto a log sticking out from the riverbank. We hauled ourselves out of the water and collapsed on the shore. Blaze's tail was singed and my left arm was bleeding badly. But we were alive - no thanks to me and my selfish quest for glory.

"This way," I gasped, heading for the canyon walls to take shelter. But the Sand Dragon wasn't finished with us just yet. The earth seemed to groan as it landed right behind us.

Its claws screeched across the rocky ground as it moved forward. It crept closer and closer, pushing us towards the canyon wall. I could see its jagged teeth and smell its charred breath. We were trapped.

This time, I knew, exhausted Blaze would struggle to run, let alone fly. Instead, though, she did something that surprised me. A ringing noise pierced the air. It came from her horn.

The dragon roared and tossed its huge head as the sound rang through the canyon. Blaze was calling for help.

Within seconds I looked up to see the sky filled with unicorns. Led by Tasha and Wildfire, the other unicorns and their riders landed on the ground shielding us from the dragon, golden light shining from their horns.

"Tash!" I cried. But she didn't hear me. All of the racers and their unicorns were focused on protecting me and Blaze. The beams of magic from their horns met overhead and formed a shimmering forcefield between us and the dragon.

The Sand Dragon howled in fury and blasted the unicorns with jets of fire, but the flames just bounced off the magical wall. The dragon clawed at the shield of light in frustration, but it held strong. As the Sand Dragon tried to burn through our defences, the Desert Flames stood united, their magic protecting us from the Sand Dragon's inferno.

"Forward!" cried Tasha.

Moving as one, the unicorns advanced, driving the Sand Dragon towards the river. As it stumbled into the water, the dragon let out a howl. Steam rose from its flanks. The unicorns pressed onwards, sensing their advantage. The dragon tried to flap its wings, but they were soaked. Soon, a wall of foam-flecked water surged into the dragon's body, sweeping it down the river.

A cheer echoed through the canyon. I threw my arms around Tasha's neck. She and the other unicorns had saved my life.

I turned to the other riders and apologized. "My foolishness cost you the race."

"There are more important things than winning, Marin," Tasha said with a smile.

I nodded, humbled by my friends' selflessness.

"Let's finish the race anyway," said Tasha.

The Desert Flames ran along the river, picking up speed, then lifted into the air. The whole herd soared over the canyon and across the desert. Just before sunset, we crossed the finish line together.

That year, there was no Desert Champion - we were all winners. In battling the Sand Dragon, we'd discovered that we were much more powerful as a team. Nothing could defeat us when we worked as one.

Where magical Woodland Flowers roam,

Mythical creatures make their home.

Forest Sprites and Imps

These creatures live deep in ancient woodlands, and even though they look friendly, they love to make magical mischief.

They blend in with trees and plants

They look deceptively sweet

Some cast spells using flowers

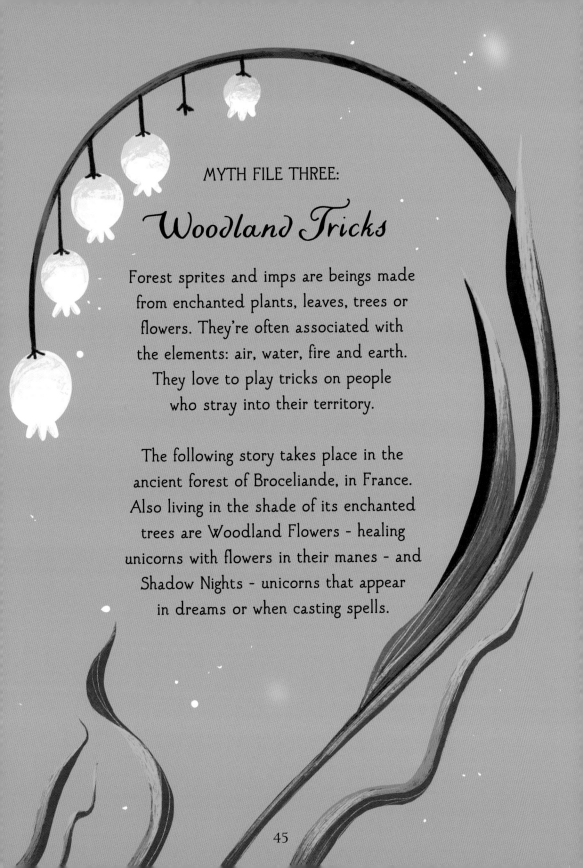

MYTH FILE THREE:

Woodland Tricks

Forest sprites and imps are beings made
from enchanted plants, leaves, trees or
flowers. They're often associated with
the elements: air, water, fire and earth.
They love to play tricks on people
who stray into their territory.

The following story takes place in the
ancient forest of Broceliande, in France.
Also living in the shade of its enchanted
trees are Woodland Flowers - healing
unicorns with flowers in their manes - and
Shadow Nights - unicorns that appear
in dreams or when casting spells.

The Shadows
of the Forest

Agnes, Beatrix and Josse lived in the north of France, not far from the enchanted Forest of Broceliande. Its ancient trees were home to all sorts of magical creatures, from the tiniest elves and fairies to the largest magical forest deer, legendary white bears and, of course, mysterious unicorns.

Most people in their village avoided the forest, but this one day, the three brave siblings had no choice but to venture inside.

"I don't like leaving him," Beatrix said, as she waded through the moss and low-lying ferns. "It doesn't feel right."

"The flower is our only hope of curing Father," Josse, her brother reminded her. "This is the only way."

"But what if we can't find it?" asked Agnes, the youngest.

Beatrix and Josse left the question hanging. Their father was gravely ill. Only sweet-balm, a beautiful flower with healing powers, could save him. They didn't want to think about what would happen if they couldn't find it.

Together, they moved between the mighty beech, pine and oak trees, searching the undergrowth for the tiny, pink flowers they needed to make a healing potion.

Fallen pine needles cushioned their footsteps and scented the air. The leaves above dappled the forest floor. If they were quiet, as quiet as they could possibly be, they might avoid disturbing the magical creatures that lived amongst the trees.

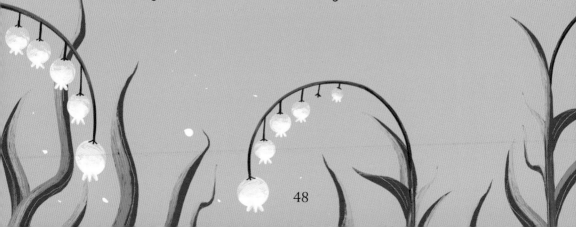

They had been trekking for hours when they came to a beautiful brook. Agnes fell to her knees. Their provisions of water had long since run out and her lips were dry with thirst. She scooped the clear, sparkling water into her hands and drank greedily.

"Blurgh!" she spat, suddenly.

What had looked like beautiful water just a moment earlier, had turned to oozing mud in her hands.

"It looked clear as glass," Agnes gasped, staring down at her muddy hands in disbelief. "I could have sworn ..."

Suddenly, from a behind a tree, they heard a peel of laughter. It sounded like a child - but the siblings knew that no children would come and play out here.

"Tee hee hee."

"Who's there?" Josse demanded. There was no reply, just the sound of rustling in the undergrowth and high-pitched laughter fading into the distance.

"A trick," said Beatrix. "We've disturbed something in the forest. We must tread more carefully from now on."

The children pressed forward, even more quiet and careful now. But it wasn't long before they heard the snap of a twig nearby. Josse squared his shoulders as if ready for a fight.

"Ah," he sighed, lowering his fists. "Look at that."

A beautiful brown unicorn stepped out from the trees. It had a pale, twisting horn and garlands of wildflowers woven into its mane and tail. Josse knew from his father's stories that it was a Woodland Flower. He had never seen such a beautiful creature.

"Can you help us find the sweet-balm flower?" he asked, moving slowly towards the majestic animal.

The unicorn bowed its head towards the ground, but in an instant, the air around it began to sparkle and the unicorn started to transform ...

"What?" Josse began.

The air, where the unicorn had been standing proudly only a moment before, came alive with a cloud of colourful moths and butterflies. The insects fluttered frantically, surrounding the three siblings.

"They're everywhere!" Agnes cried.

Then, just as quickly as they appeared, the butterflies and moths flew off into the trees all around them.

Once again, laughter rang out from the trees.

"Tee hee hee."

The siblings exchanged worried glances.

"Something very strange is going on," said Agnes. "I think we should go home."

"We've come too far," Beatrix said, shaking her head. "We can't turn back now."

"Think of Father," Josse added.

Beatrix nodded. "Something is hiding in these trees, making mischief with us. I've heard of creatures that can do this - sprites and imps made of pure forest magic that confuse and trick anyone who cross their paths. They're only small, but they're very annoying. We need to perform a spell. Father always said that we could count on unicorn magic to help in times of trouble. Shadow Nights protect people, don't they? It's worth trying."

Beatrix grabbed hold of her siblings' hands and formed a circle. She began chanting magic, calling upon the ancient powers of unicorns to protect them. They whirled around the forest clearing and spoke in unison:

"Shadow Night, keep us safe, banish hidden harm,
Use your shadow magic, your wisdom and your calm."

With the spell cast, they wasted no time resuming their search for the flower. Though, after a time, the rumbling of their bellies grew louder, even louder than the laughter that seemed to follow their every move.

Agnes spotted some mushrooms growing around the trunk of a huge oak tree. The three hungry siblings ran towards them eagerly - and then stopped. The mushrooms were glowing with an ominous green light. Next, they spotted a blackberry bush full to bursting with ripe fruit. But the blackberries were emitting a strange glow, too.

"It's the sprites' magic," Beatrix said. "And now, since we called upon the magic of the Shadow Night, we can see it!"

The three siblings backed away from the sinister-looking mushrooms and blackberries, even though they were desperately hungry. Instead of the usual laughing and giggling from the trees, they heard nothing but disgruntled moans.

"See," said Agnes. "The sprites are annoyed that we haven't fallen into their trap!"

As soon as she'd spoken, a tiny elfin creature, that looked like the bark of a tree, peeked out from behind a bush. It tiptoed up to Agnes and stuck out its tongue, giggling.

"Tee hee hee."

"Hello," said Agnes calmly, determined not to be afraid.

It frowned, then, and scurried back into the trees.

Next, two sprites fluttered into the clearing. One pinched Josse with sharp little fingers, while the other tugged on Beatrix's long, blonde hair.

"Stop that," said Josse, batting a sprite away.

The creature gave an indignant shriek and called for back-up. Imps with pointed ears and wide, mischievous eyes crept out of the forest. Sprites with gossamer wings and dresses made from cobwebs flew down from the treetops.

"What sorcery do you possess that can resist our tricks?" shrieked an angry sprite, the leader of the tribe. "How do you know to avoid our magic?"

"By the power of unicorns," Beatrix said, grinning. "They always keep travellers safe in these woods."

The imps and sprites frowned and began to close in on the siblings. Imps pelted them with acorns and chestnuts. Sprites annoyed them from above, pulling at their hair and hitting them with sticks. It was more playful and mischievous than anything else, but the siblings couldn't help but be annoyed.

"Beatrix, do something." Josse said. "They're getting on my nerves."

Quickly, Beatrix grabbed the others' hands and formed the circle once more, and let out a cry into the forest:

> *"The forest teems with imps and sprites,*
> *Protect us quickly, Shadow Night!"*

Suddenly, a glittering mist rolled into the clearing and out of it stepped a Shadow Night unicorn. Stars sparkled on its black body like constellations in the night sky. With a sharp neigh, the Shadow Night shook its mane and galloped around the clearing. Tiny silver stars flew off its body and floated through the air like magical dust, coating the elves and sprites. Instantly drowsy, the woodland creatures yawned and rubbed their eyes. One by one, they curled up on the forest floor and began to snore.

"It worked!" cried Agnes. "Look, they're all asleep."

Beatrix walked up to the Shadow Night and stroked its long nose.

"Thank you," she whispered.

The unicorn tossed its head and beckoned for them to follow. It led them to a patch of ivy, then lowered its onyx horn to point at some delicate pink flowers hidden among the vines.

"Sweet-balm!" exclaimed Beatrix. She and her siblings quickly picked as many blossoms as they could hold.

When they turned to say goodbye to the Shadow Night, it was no longer there. The unicorn had vanished without a trace; not even a hoofprint remained.

It felt like a dream, but Agnes, Beatrix and Josse never doubted that the unicorn had been real. They felt its presence with them still, as they hurried through the woods, carrying the precious plants. This time, no laughter followed them. No imps played tricks. No sprites caused trouble. The Shadow Night's magic protected them all the way home to the safety of their village.

Kraken

The Kraken lives deep in the icy waters of the Arctic Ocean.
It is a nightmarish, squid-like creature, full of raw power.

A large brain
that makes it
clever and cunning

Huge eyes
for seeing
in the dark

MYTH FILE FOUR:

Ocean Terror

Ever since sailors have ventured
out onto the open waters, there
have been tales of this terrifying
creature lurking in the deep.

The Kraken has strong tentacles that
it uses to crush its prey and keen
vision to peer through dark waters.
As this old diary from an M.U.S.
researcher shows, it shares its home
with Water Moons, helpful unicorns
that live on, and in, water.

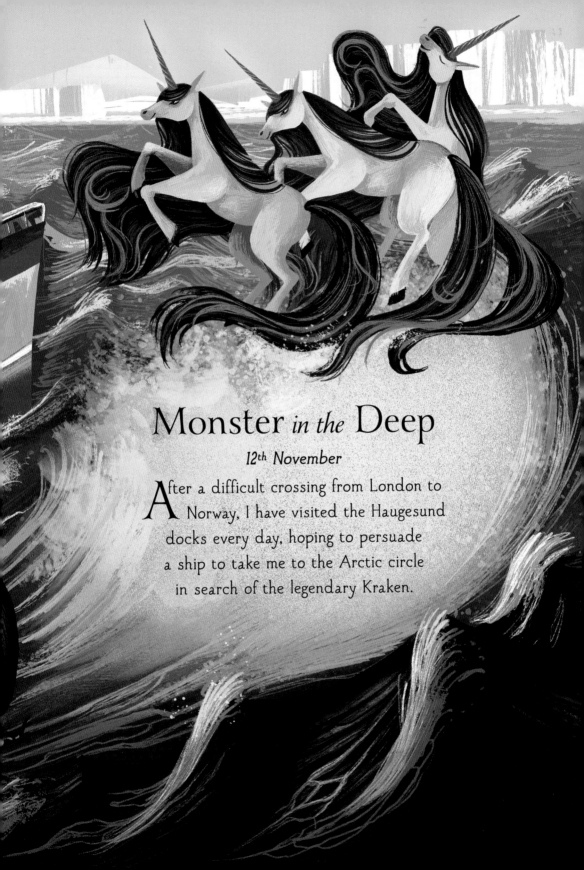

Monster *in the* Deep

12th November

After a difficult crossing from London to Norway, I have visited the Haugesund docks every day, hoping to persuade a ship to take me to the Arctic circle in search of the legendary Kraken.

Most of the captains just laughed in my face, while others looked frightened and warned me to abandon my plan to locate this infamous sea monster. But today, aided by a letter of introduction from the Magical Unicorn Society, I finally secured my passage and boarded *The Kelpie*, a fishing trawler heading back to its home port of Nova Scotia in Canada. Its white-bearded captain, Angus O'Hara agreed to take a detour through the Greenland Strait, though he warned me that the trip would not be easy "for a landlubber".

Little does he know that I, Elizabeth Walker, have endured far more challenging journeys researching mythical creatures, and that I would not be deterred by a few big waves.

The rest of the crew do not seem as enthusiastic as the captain. The cook scowled at me as he dished out my dinner and I heard the first mate muttering ominously about "foolish tourists".

Happily, it turns out that I am not the only paying customer on board. Frank Barnes, a merchant seaman, joined the expedition, bound for Canada. He's a friendly, interesting fellow, and I am glad of his company.

14th November

I apologize for not writing yesterday. I admit that the seas were indeed a bit rough and my stomach churned like the waves outside my porthole. It seems O'Hara had a point. Confined to my small cabin, I decided to study the books that inspired me to make the journey. The Vikings were the first to tell stories about a monster that haunted the northernmost seas, but there have been other sightings through the years. Some tell of a colossal octopus with a bulbous head the size of a bus, and a gaping mouth big enough to swallow a ship whole. Others describe a creature with fierce, bulging eyes and long tentacles covered with suckers the size of dinner plates. What all the accounts agree on, however, is that the Kraken is very, very dangerous indeed.

Feeling much better today, I bundled myself into my oilskin coat and braved the slippery deck. I spent long and dreary hours in the sea spray, scanning the waves with my telescope for any sign of the beast. The icy wind stung my cheeks and made my eyes water. Fortunately, Barnes brought me hot coffee and kept me company as I gazed out over the grey horizon. To my great surprise, he asked me if it was true that Water Moon unicorns live in these icy waters. I was amazed, for few people have ever heard of these elusive water-dwelling creatures, with their stunning blue coats and sapphire horns. Before I had a chance to speak, I saw a large shape appear on the horizon. Too big to be a whale. Bigger, even, than another ship. In the blink of an eye, it sank below the waterline. Was my imagination running wild? Or had I just spotted the Kraken?

15th November

Today there can be no doubt ... I saw the Kraken! Through my telescope, I watched as it emerged from the sea to slap an iceberg out of its way with one enormous, slimy tentacle. I thought I saw something else there, too. A blue light glinting in the distance. Could it have been a unicorn horn?

I dashed to the bridge to tell Captain O'Hara the news and asked him to steer the ship north in pursuit. Fearful of a mutiny, the first mate tried to persuade the captain not to follow the beast. The crew were uneasy, their minds filled with superstitions and shipwrecks.

The longer we debated, the further away the Kraken was getting. In the end, Barnes reminded the captain of our deal. The captain turned the wheel and we headed north, towards the Greenland Strait. I am so grateful to have an ally such as Barnes onboard.

16th November

As we pursue the sea beast, icebergs rise like ghosts from
the dark water. Icicles form in the sailors' beards as they
swab the decks. Although my nose is frostbitten and my
fingertips are numb, I am warmed by the knowledge that
I am doing important work for the Magical Unicorn Society.
All day long, I peer through my telescope, sketching the Kraken
and jotting down notes on its habits. I am slowly beginning to
understand this mysterious creature. In the morning, it hunts,
opening its cavernous, stinking mouth and devouring whole
seals. It disappears into the depths in the afternoon and,
come evening, it reappears full of energy and movement.

Although my work is going well, something troubles me. This
afternoon, as I made my way to the galley to scrounge some
ship's biscuits, I heard whispers coming from the captain's cabin.
I hid behind a pile of fishing nets and listened to the voices of
the captain and my friend, Barnes. Captain O'Hara said he was
worried about taking the boat through such treacherous waters.
In a threatening tone I have never heard him use before, Barnes
reminded the captain of the fortune they would both make. I
distinctly heard him say: "She's leading us right there." I am the
only female onboard, apart from Greta, the cook's cat. Could it
be that I am not the only one searching for something?

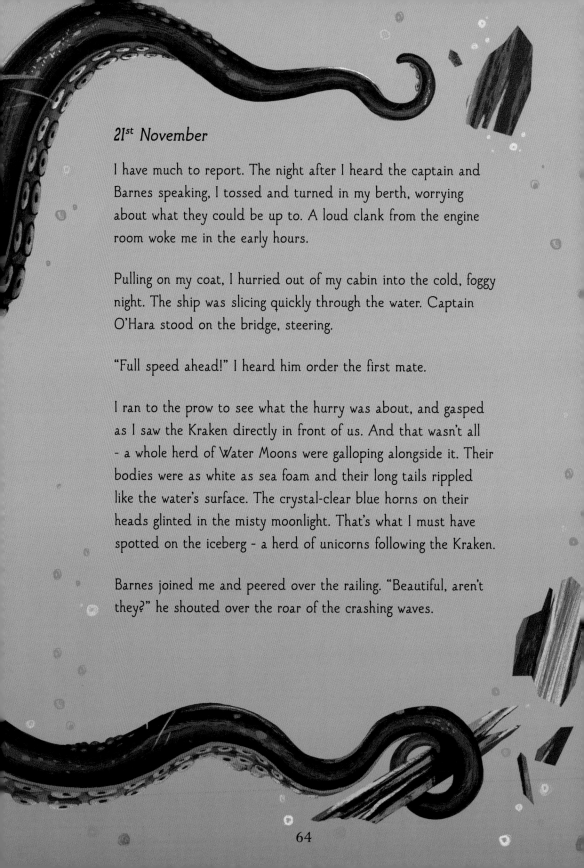

21st November

I have much to report. The night after I heard the captain and
Barnes speaking, I tossed and turned in my berth, worrying
about what they could be up to. A loud clank from the engine
room woke me in the early hours.

Pulling on my coat, I hurried out of my cabin into the cold, foggy
night. The ship was slicing quickly through the water. Captain
O'Hara stood on the bridge, steering.

"Full speed ahead!" I heard him order the first mate.

I ran to the prow to see what the hurry was about, and gasped
as I saw the Kraken directly in front of us. And that wasn't all
- a whole herd of Water Moons were galloping alongside it. Their
bodies were as white as sea foam and their long tails rippled
like the water's surface. The crystal-clear blue horns on their
heads glinted in the misty moonlight. That's what I must have
spotted on the iceberg - a herd of unicorns following the Kraken.

Barnes joined me and peered over the railing. "Beautiful, aren't
they?" he shouted over the roar of the crashing waves.

"Yes," I agreed. But Barnes seemed so unsurprised at seeing these magnificent creatures that I was perplexed. "What do you know about unicorns?"

What he said to me took me back.

"I know that they fetch a high price."

The blood in my veins chilled.

"I trade in magical creatures," he continued. "These Water Moons are some of the rarest and most valuable of them all. When I heard of a voyage to the far north to look for the Kraken I had to join. You must know that where the Kraken leads, Water Moons aren't far behind. Really, I have to thank you, Elizabeth. You've led me straight to them."

I stepped back from the railing. So that was his plan. Barnes would try to capture the unicorns and sell them to the highest bidder. I had played into his hands and led him right to them.

"You'll never get away with it," I spat. "I'll stop you!"

But just then, the ship slowed and Captain O'Hara ordered the crew to lower rowing boats loaded with nets into the water.

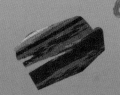

I begged him to stop. The Water Moons would never survive in captivity, caged and reduced to being nothing but exotic trophies. But he ignored me.

As a deckhand turned the crank to lower the boats, I tackled him to the deck. The captain ordered the crew to seize me and rough hands dragged me away. Captain O'Hara began turning the crank himself, but it was frozen stiff. Frustrated, he pulled a knife out of his pocket and slashed at the rope, sending the boat crashing into the sea.

From below us came an enraged bellow from the gaping mouth of the Kraken. Its bulbous purple head, bleeding from where the boat had hit it, rose out of the water and loomed over the deck. For the first time I could fully appreciate just how huge the Kraken was. Its eyes glowered with a thirst for revenge.

"Captain!" cried the first mate, "What do we do?"

Tentacles, longer than the ship itself, whipped through the air and the Kraken scooped up The Kelpie as if it was merely a bath toy. I clung to a metal railing as the ship groaned and creaked. Cries of terror filled the air as the Kraken tightened its grip, and with a sickening crunch, the ship broke in two ...

I went flying through the air, the cries of a dozen men all around me. I will never forget the shock of cold as I plunged into the freezing water. I flailed, fighting for life, as my heavy, waterlogged clothes dragged me down towards the ocean floor. But just as my lungs were about to burst, the glowing white shape of a Water Moon pranced through the dark water towards me. I threw my arms around the unicorn's neck - as did other sailors in the depths around me - and it swam back up to the surface. The Water Moon who had rescued me set me down gently on an ice floe. It lay down beside me, covering my shivering body with its long mane.

The sailors and I were not only saved from the depths by the Water Moons, they also kept us alive on the freezing ice with the warmth of their bodies until dawn broke. Eventually, a passing cargo ship rescued us and carried us safely to Canada, where I write this now.

Captain O'Hara and Barnes were never found, but the rest of *The Kelpie*'s crew were saved. The newspapers are calling it a miracle. But those of us who survived that night know that it wasn't a miracle that saved us - it was the magic of the Water Moon unicorns.

While the world is lost in sleep,

Magical creatures roam the deep.

Stone Troll

Stone trolls lurk in mountain caves across the world. They crave gold and jewels, and are fiercely protective of their hoards.

Crown of
solid gold

Muscles made
of solid rock

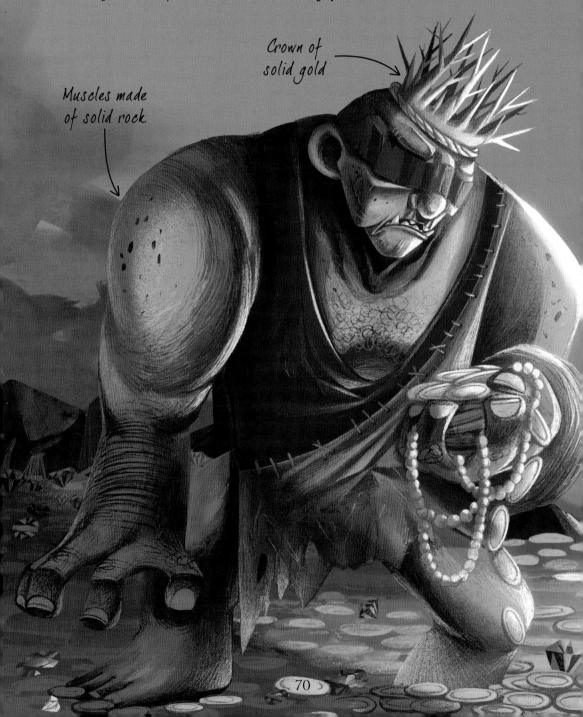

MYTH FILE FIVE:

Hidden Riches

Stone trolls are entities made of rock,
stone and magic. They can be found in
mountain caves, on rocky moorlands
and even in underwater volcanoes.

They have a range of powers, from brute
strength to use of elemental magic. Some
types of stone troll want nothing more
than gold, jewels and gems, like the ones
found in the Himalayan mountains.

The following story was told to me by a goat
herder on my travels through this beautiful
region. It also features Mountain Jewel unicorns,
which are known for being hardy and loyal.

The Jewels
of the Mountain

A deep rumble boomed through the cave. The walls of the chamber began to tremble and the floor shook. I was thrown off my unicorn and straight onto the hard stone floor, along with several of the king's men around me.

The pile of gold and jewels in front of us - taller than ten elephants and wider than a palace hall - began to tumble forward like a tidal wave.

"Earthquake?" I cried, clambering to my feet.

The king and his men looked around frantically. It wasn't an earthquake. The rumbling came from the mound of golden coins in front of us, from which the nightmarish figure of a giant, stinking, stone troll emerged. It was mean, filthy, powerful and enraged. Its muscles were the size of boulders, its huge head leered at us and its fists swung around heavily like battering rams ready to burst through a door.

King Oro and his guards got back to their feet and faced the monstrosity in front of them. But the troll simply laughed. And, in a voice so loud it echoed through the mountain, it cried:

"Who DARES steal my treasure?"

I took a step backwards, all the better to avoid the troll's rocky bulk, and braced myself. I had no idea what would happen next ...

*

It had all started that morning in the king's stables, far down the mountain's slopes. King Oro and his men were planning an expedition high into the mountains to look for gold and jewels. I had come to join it. The people of our kingdom had always lived in poverty - if we went along, we would be handsomely rewarded.

"Ready, Norbu?" I asked my unicorn.

Norbu stamped his shaggy hooves on the ground in reply. Mountain Jewel unicorns are famously strong, hardy, graceful and loyal. Norbu would stand by me, whatever happened.

I slipped a bridle over his head, then led him into the stable yard, where the rest of our scrawny band of volunteers had assembled and my friend, Sonam, was waiting.

"At last!" Sonam beamed. "Time to get that treasure, Jinpa."

"It is," I replied, "And lots of it, too, I hope!"

We hadn't been in the courtyard long, when the king emerged. Flanked by guards wearing pointed helmets and copper armour, Oro strode forward. He wore a white brocade tunic and had a curving gold sword that made him stand out from all the other men around him.

"Your bravery will save our kingdom from poverty," he boomed. "Together we will reclaim the gold that is rightfully ours!"

The assembled gang cheered.

There was just one thing that bothered me in that moment: the king's appearance. Many of us had never seen him in person and we were always told that he was a humble man. From the provisions we saw being stored in his saddlebags and his obviously-expensive garments, that clearly wasn't the case.

Nevertheless, there wasn't time to dwell on these matters. We were all encouraged to quickly mount our unicorns and set off towards the snow-capped peak in the distance.

*

After hours of trekking, we reached a door carved into the mountainside. The Mountain Jewels we were riding slowed down and some even began to paw at the ground.

"The unicorns sense we're near treasure," said King Oro.

I nudged Norbu and steered him through the doorway behind the king's men and the volunteers. He knew just where to go, even when the cave became a labyrinth of winding passages.

Gradually, the darkness gave way to a glimmer of light and we reached a magnificent chamber. I had to put a hand in front of my eyes to shield them from the sparkling mass of gold coins, emeralds, sapphires and rubies. No one in our kingdom's history had seen a mound of riches such as this.

"Wow!" Sonam gasped. "It's like a mountain in itself."

Ahead, King Oro jumped down from his unicorn and buried his hands in the gems. He grabbed handfuls of gold and let it trickle through his fingers like a waterfall.

"At last!" he cried, desperately. "All this will be mine!"

Mine? I thought, confused. *Ours, surely?*

But that's when the stone troll emerged.

*

I picked myself up from the floor, just as a huge, stone fist came crashing down beside me. Sonam reached out his hand and pulled me up out the way of danger. Norbu was near, too, rearing up with his powerful, Mountain Jewel legs. Sparks flew in the air as his hooves scraped against the troll's stone body.

"Norbu, get back!" I cried.

The stone troll staggered around the chamber, lashing out wildly. But quickly, he seemed to tire, and soon I came to understand why.

There'd been a thin, red bandage wrapped around his head before, but in all the commotion it had fallen from his face to reveal two empty craters where his eyes should have been. The stone troll was blind. He couldn't see any of us.

"Blinded by the glare of your own riches," King Oro laughed. "Fill your packs with as much gold as you can carry, men. My palace will soon be the envy of the world!"

The king's men moved forward, but the stone troll wasn't going to give up without a fight. Sitting atop his mound of treasure, he uttered a curse that echoed across the chamber.

> *"These men have come to steal my gold,*
> *Stop them now, magic of old!"*

Suddenly, gold coins flew up into the air. Then, they shot out in every direction, striking some of the king's men who, unlike the volunteers, were already stuffing their pockets with gold. Once hit, the men grew sluggish and slow until, amazingly, they began to turn into golden statues right in front of our eyes.

A coin flew at me and I ducked. Another came whizzing from the opposite direction and Norbu flicked it away with his horn. King Oro raised his shield, battering away the magical gold coins.

"Take all my men!" he shouted, panicking. "Turn them to gold if you will. Just let me live!"

It was clear now that the king cared nothing for us - only his own vanity and wealth. The king's men who hadn't been turned to gold tried to flee. The volunteers were way ahead of them, racing back out the chamber.

"It's too late for that," said the troll, magic pulsing out from all around him. A bolt of energy shot forth from his hands, rooting the king to the spot. "But I *will* give you a chance to escape with your life."

"Anything," the cowardly king, cried.

"Solve my riddle and my treasure will be yours," the troll cried. "If you cannot, you will turn into the gold you love so much."

King Oro, stuck to the spot by the troll's magic, had no choice but to agree.

"Tell me this," began the troll, striding forward.

"What is an empty void that gold can never fill,
Without which, you'll live a life of goodwill?"

King Oro scratched his head. He looked at his men desperately, hoping to find the answer somewhere.

"Time's nearly up," chuckled the troll.

"I–I–I don't know!" the King cried.

"He should," I muttered to Sonam. "The answer's GREED."

The troll moved forwards, magic pulsing in between his hands. In a flash, it burst forth, striking the king in his chest.

"NOO!" he shouted.

I swung myself onto Norbu's back and pulled Sonam up on the saddle behind me. Unicorns, some with riders on their backs and some without, galloped out of the chamber.

I looked over my shoulder and saw King Oro on his hands and knees, desperately scooping up coins and jewels, even as, at the very same moment, he slowly turned to solid gold.

"Let's go!" I shouted to Norbu, racing out of the chamber.

Just then, a powerful magic from the stone troll burst forth, like a volcano erupting. Rocks, gems and coins flew through the air.

Norbu raced through the labyrinth and the whole mountain range shook with the stone troll's red-hot fury as we burst into the daylight. A moment later, the vast doors in the mountainside slammed shut, trapping the king, and the greediest of his men, inside their golden tomb forever.

I gulped the crisp air. My saddle bags were empty, but that didn't matter. I was still alive. And so were all the brave Mountain Jewels and the volunteers.

The aftershocks of the stone troll's magic were felt far and wide. When we returned home, the palace lay in ruins. Gold and jewels glittered among the rubble. Behind the palace's plain walls, King Oro had stockpiled treasure, paid for with our toil. We weren't really poor - it was our king that had been consumed with greed.

The king's treasure was distributed equally among everyone in the realm. From that day forward, our people never went hungry again. Our generous land provided us with everything we needed to live a good and honest life. We never forgot the valuable lesson we learned that day: that a greedy man is always poor.

Phoenix

These birds were once thought to only exist in ancient myths,
but they have recently been discovered in real life.

Fire-breathing
beak

Feathers made
of fire

Sharp claws for
grappling other
mythical creatures

MYTH FILE SIX:

Flame Birds

A large part of the phoenix's
story is already known from ancient
myths. It is said that when one dies,
it bursts into flame, and another rises
from the ashes to take its place.

But they are also associated with
creatures entirely their opposite: Ice
Wanderer unicorns. These unicorns
live in the coldest places on Earth,
and are some of the hardiest
creatures we know about.

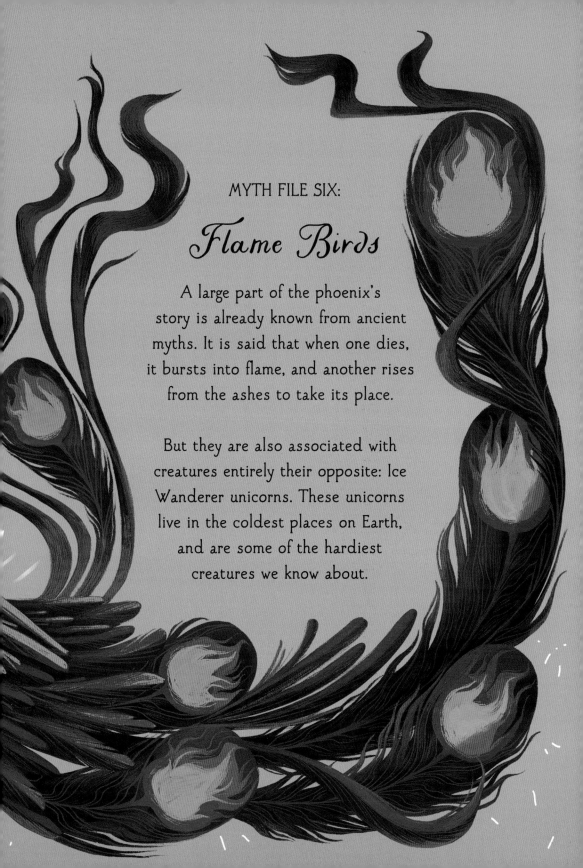

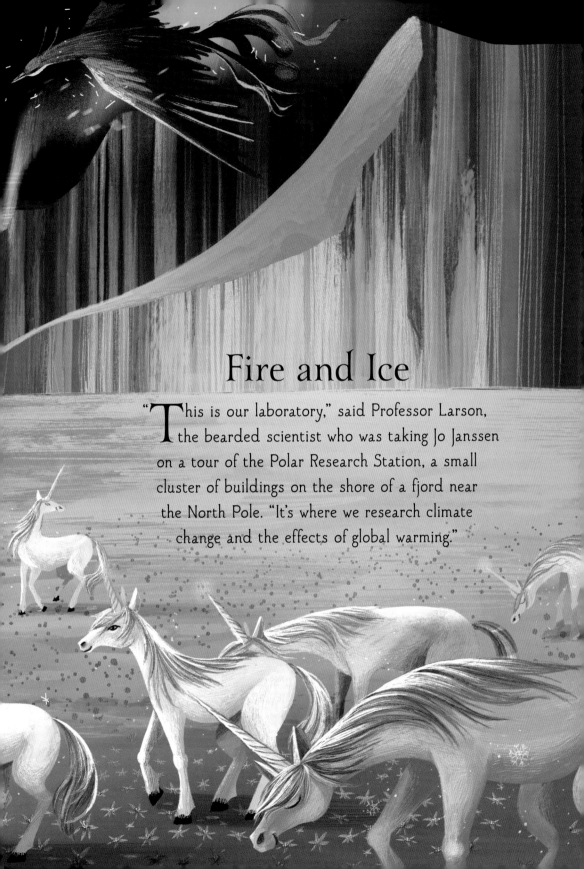

Fire and Ice

"This is our laboratory," said Professor Larson, the bearded scientist who was taking Jo Janssen on a tour of the Polar Research Station, a small cluster of buildings on the shore of a fjord near the North Pole. "It's where we research climate change and the effects of global warming."

"We study the area's plant life and monitor the populations
of Arctic animals," said his colleague, Dr Anna Medvedova.
"Orcas, seals, polar bears ... and other creatures," she finished.

Jo Janssen nodded politely. The high-tech lab equipment was
very impressive, but it wasn't the reason she had come to the
Arctic circle. The scientists thought she was a journalist, writing
an article on the research station's work. But the real reason
she'd come was to catch a glimpse of an Ice Wanderer unicorn.

Back at the Magical Unicorn Society's Department of Myths
and Monsters, Jo had studied everything she could about these
hardy unicorns that lived in the world's coldest climates. Their
sparkling white coats protected them from the elements and,
although they were solitary creatures, they communicated with
other unicorns across vast distances by beaming light from their
pearly horns. Sightings of Ice Wanderers were incredibly rare,
but Jo was determined to track one down.

The scientists led her into a dome-shaped observatory with
glass walls. Computer screens blinked with satellite images.
Outside the windows, Jo could see a glacier of blue-tinged ice
spilling into the fjord like a frozen waterfall.

"This is where we study polar weather conditions," said Anna.

Jo looked out at the icebergs floating in the water. She spotted a long, white horn in amongst the floes. Her heart skipped a beat.

"A narwhal," Anna said, following Jo's gaze. "Did you know they're actually whales, though some people call them sea unicorns?"

"Oh, of course," Jo replied, feeling foolish for thinking she might have found an Ice Wanderer so quickly. "It's funny, for a moment I thought it might be a real unicorn. There's a type up here with horns that light up the night sky, I believe ... "

Professor Larson snorted. "The Northern Lights are caused by electrically charged particles from space entering the atmosphere. Those are the only lights you'll find in the skies up here."

"I've read tales about phoenixes, too," Jo persisted. "Fiery birds whose flames melt the ice."

"We are scientists," Larson scoffed. "We're not interested in myths and legends here." Still chuckling, he went into his office.

But Anna Medvedova wasn't laughing. She stared at Jo intently.

"Do you want to come on a field trip with me?" she asked. "There's a place I know you might find interesting ... "

*

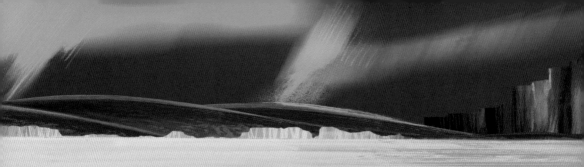

An hour later, Jo and Anna were shooting across the tundra
on a snowmobile, heading north. Even though she was bundled
up, Jo could still feel the icy wind cutting into her. Eventually
they stopped to set up camp. Jo shivered as the wind whistled
across the frozen landscape, battering the sides of the tent.

"You're not really a journalist, are you?" Anna asked, as they
made dinner. "You are searching for unicorns, I think."

"Yes," admitted Jo. "I work for the Magical Unicorn Society. I
came here in hopes of studying Ice Wanderer unicorns."

"I grew up in Siberia, in the north of Russia," Anna said. "My
grandmother used to tell me stories about snow unicorns, and
the battles they fought against their enemies, the phoenixes."

Jo listened intently. She'd read stories like that herself in the
Magical Unicorn Society's library.

"Why do they fight?" she asked.

"They represent two opposing forces of nature. Phoenix feathers
are made of pure fire. The Ice Wanderers thrive in the ice.
When they meet, they come together in battle. I, too, thought
my grandmother's stories were only myths, but I've been
studying satellite images from the lab. I've noticed some strange

atmospheric activity that science alone cannot explain."

"Go on," Jo urged.

"Every year, when the pink snow daisies are in bloom, the night sky fills with even more light than usual," Anna explained.

"What do you think it means?" asked Jo, unable to keep the excitement out of her voice.

"My colleagues would scoff if they heard me saying this," said Anna. "But I suspect unicorns come to graze on the flowers."

Ice Wanderers! thought Jo. It had to be. "What are we waiting for?" she cried. "Let's go!"

Anna took out a device and entered in some coordinates. "The daisies grow due north of here," she explained. "The terrain is too rough for the snowmobile - we'll have to travel there on foot."

They strapped on snowshoes and headed out into the cold night. Starlight reflected on the snow, making it bright enough to see their way. The only sound to be heard was their panting breath as they hiked across the hard crust of snow. At the top of a steep drift, they came to an abrupt stop. Below them lay a valley carpeted in tiny flowers, turning the snow pink.

"Snow daisies," explained Anna. She pointed at the sky and traced a shape in the stars with her finger. "Can you see the constellation of stars that looks like a unicorn?"

Jo gazed up at the twinkling sky and nodded.

"I've studied the data, and the flowers only blossom when the stars align in that position."

Suddenly, a streak of purple light danced across the night sky. An answering beam of green came shooting from the opposite direction. Pink light flashed across the darkness, and a yellow beam whizzed past in reply. Jo stared in wonder as colourful light painted the heavens with magical glowing swirls.

"Look!" whispered Jo, clutching Anna's arm. Out of nowhere, unicorns had appeared among the flowers below.

There had to be at least thirty of them, their white coats twinkling with icy magic as they grazed on the snow daisies.

"I've got to get a better look at them," said Jo.

"Be careful," warned Anna. "The snow might not be stable."

But Jo was already scrambling down the slope. The chance to study the Ice Wanderers up close was too good to resist.

By the time she reached the bottom of the slope, she felt warm for the first time since she'd arrived in the Arctic. Looking up, she saw that a red glow had filled the sky.

An enormous flock of red birds circled overhead, their flame-coloured wings spread wide. Then, without warning, a bird swooped down and attacked one of the unicorns. It breathed ribbons of fire out of its sharp beak and, around the unicorn, the snow began to melt.

The Ice Wanderer reared up and slammed its hooves into the snow. Sparkling ice crystals flew off its coat, swirling through the air and extinguishing the phoenix's fiery breath.

The smoking bird spiralled through the sky before crashing to the ground and dissolving into a pile of ashes.

As Jo watched in amazement, the phoenix was reborn - clawing its way out of the ashes and soaring back in the air. It let out an ear-piercing shriek and rejoined the other phoenixes in the air. The phoenixes and unicorns began to do battle - and Jo was caught in the middle. Phoenixes scratched at the unicorns with their claws and blasted fire from their beaks, scorching the snow. The unicorns fought the birds off with their horns and retaliated with blizzards of snow.

Jo could barely see through the chaos. Hailstones stung her cheeks. She ducked as a phoenix swooped past, so close its feathers brushed her head, singing her hair. Suddenly, the snow around her began to melt, puddling at her feet. There was a loud rumble as the slope thawed and snow raced down the hill.

"Avalanche!" she cried.

Terror rooted her to the spot as a wave of snow fell down. Just before it engulfed her, a unicorn galloped to the rescue. Icy blue light shot out of its horn, freezing the snow again and stopping the avalanche in its tracks.

"Thank you," Jo gasped in relief.

The Ice Wanderer lowered its head in acknowledgement and darted back into battle with a swish of its golden tail.

Jo clambered back up the frozen slope and Anna pulled her to safety. The two women watched silently as the battle between fire and ice raged through the night.

By dawn, the unicorns had chased the phoenixes away, sending them flying towards the rising sun. Gradually, the exhausted unicorns drifted away, each in a different direction, returning to their solitary existence. They would not reunite until the flowers blossomed again.

"That was amazing," said Jo, breathlessly.

The early morning sky was as pink as the flowers in the snow. The lingering smell of smoke was the only hint of the battle that had just been fought between the powerful forces of nature.

"Without the Ice Wanderers, this polar ice cap would have melted," said Anna. "And the danger is worse than ever now that global warming affects the ice."

"You should tell your colleagues that unicorns are playing their part," said Jo.

Anna laughed. "Professor Larson would never believe me!"

"Maybe he will if you have proof," said Jo. She picked up a phoenix feather that had fallen on the ground, its vivid red staining the snow like a drop of blood.

But as she held it in her palm, it turned to ash.

There was no evidence to show for what she had witnessed that night. But for as long as she lived, Jo would never forget that spectacular battle of the elements - or the unicorn that had saved her life.

Under starry skies and full moon bright,

Unicorns play through the night.

Werewolf

Werewolves are cursed human beings who shapeshift into fearsome wolves at the time of the full moon.

Sharp teeth and piercing red eyes

Large claws and strong muscles

MYTH FILE SEVEN:

By Moonlight

A person gains the power to transform from a human to a wolf after they have been bitten by another werewolf. The transformation is activated by the light of the full moon.

They are strong, powerful and fierce creatures, with blood-curdling howls that send fear into the hearts of even the bravest people. But they have a rival in the form of Storm Chasers. These amazing unicorns can channel the forces of lightning, thunder, storms and rain, to protect themselves and others from harm as in this tale from ancient Greece.

The Perfect Storm

Long ago, in ancient Greece, there lived a peasant boy named Petros. His family had a small flock of sheep, and every day Petros led them up into the foothills of Mount Olympus to graze.

He lived in an old farmhouse, perched on the side of the mountain, with his mother and father. One morning, Petros's mother discovered that a jug of ewe's milk, fresh just the day before, had curdled overnight.

"This is a bad omen," she said, her brows creasing into a frown.

"It is indeed," said Petros's father. "There will be a storm tonight, you can be sure."

Petros glanced out of the window. It was a bright morning, with clear blue skies, and he couldn't see any signs of bad weather.

"How do you know?" he asked.

"We're due a full moon, too," Petros's mother said. "Combined with the curdled milk, something bad is surely brewing."

"Mark my words," said his father. "We'll hear the sound of Storm Chasers' hooves tonight."

People in Petros's village believed that thunder was caused by Storm Chaser unicorns - magical creatures with a deep connection to the weather - galloping through the mountains. But that wasn't all: they also believed that werewolves prowled the mountainside when the moon was at its fullest.

Apparently werewolves looked just like ordinary people. But during the full moon, they would transform, becoming ferocious wolves. If they bit a human during this time, their victim would be cursed to share the same affliction.

"Be sure to bring the flock home before nightfall," Petros's mother said, nervously.

"Of course," Petros said. "We'll be back before dark."

Petros whistled for his dog, Hercules, then headed out. He let the sheep out of the barn and they made their way up the mountainside to graze. Petros hummed to himself happily as he watched the lambs gambolling in the morning sunshine.

As they passed an olive grove, though, Hercules stopped dead in his tracks and growled. A stranger stepped out from between the trees. He had an unkempt beard, bloodshot eyes and wore dirty, tattered clothes.

"Are you lost?" Petros asked him.

The man just shook his head and grinned, showing his yellow teeth. His eyes flashed an unearthly red.

Petros felt the hairs on the back of his neck prickle. The man

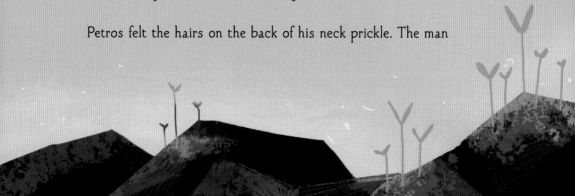

had a wild look he didn't trust. Not wanting to hang around, he whistled to Hercules, and they hurried onwards.

When at last they reached a fresh pasture, Petros sat on a rock and watched his flock. But he couldn't shake the image of the man lurking in the mountainside. He pulled out his knife and a small piece of olive wood and began to whittle the wood into the shape of a horse. Then, he carved a horn, turning it into a unicorn. He knew that unicorns' powerful magic could cause storms and control weather, but that they also offered protection, too. He felt like he might need a lucky charm.

Putting the wooden unicorn in the pouch on his belt, he took out some bread and a lump of cheese and ate his lunch. By now, the sun was high in the sky. Insects buzzed in the hazy midday heat. Even the friskiest lambs had curled up next to their mothers for an afternoon nap, so Petros decided to do the same. He settled under the shade of a cedar tree and closed his eyes. Soon, he was fast asleep.

He woke with a start, hours later. The blue sky had turned grey and the humid air felt charged with electricity. Remembering his father's warning about the storm, Petros scrambled to his feet and whistled for Hercules. They rounded up the sheep just as a strong wind began to blow, whipping the trees' branches.

Petros did a quick count of the sheep and discovered that one of the lambs, Delphi, was missing.

"Delphi!" he shouted. "Delphi, where are you?" He searched the whole pasture but couldn't find the lamb anywhere.

Alarmed, Petros saw that darkness was falling. The full moon was peeking out from behind heavy grey clouds. The flock bleated nervously, sensing the brewing storm. There would be just enough time to get them back to the village before the rain started, but Petros couldn't leave Delphi on her own all night. A wolf would surely get her.

Petros quickly herded the flock into a cave in the mountainside and left Hercules in charge of guarding over them. In the distance, he heard what sounded like wolves howling. He shivered, hoping it was his mind playing tricks on him, and he forced himself out into the night.

"Delphi!" he called, desperately.

He climbed further up the mountain, where there was another pasture. Over the wind, he heard the faint sound of bleating. Petros followed the sound and, to his relief, found Delphi tangled in a patch of thistles, the plant's spiky burrs caught in her wool.

"There you are," he said, stroking the lamb's head. "Don't wander so far from the flock next time, eh?"

However, just as Petros worked to free the lamb, he heard a voice behind him.

"We meet again," it said.

Petros spun around and saw the scruffy stranger he'd encountered that morning. This time, Petros knew for certain that there was evil in his eyes. The man stepped forwards, and just then the clouds moved away from the moon and its light shone down. The man threw his head back, howled and, incredibly, his body began to change.

His back hunched and his yellow teeth became long fangs. His fingernails grew into sharp claws. Pointed ears appeared either side of his head and thick fur sprouted all over his body. He howled again and dropped onto all fours, his transformation into a werewolf complete.

Petros took a step back, gulping down his fear.

From the mountainside came more howls. Yellow eyes appeared all around them, other, normal wolves, drawn by the werewolf, crept out of the darkness, circling their prey.

"Get back!" Petros cried, stepping forward bravely and shielding the lamb with his body. He fumbled in his pouch, trying to find his knife. Instead, his fingers grasped the wooden unicorn he'd carved earlier. He was shocked to find that it was hot. He took it out of his pocket. The wooden trinket he'd carved just hours ago was glowing.

Suddenly, a bolt of lightning lit up the sky. In the flash of light, Petros could see the werewolf's tongue lolling hungrily and the whites of his eyes rolling wildly. He squeezed the wooden unicorn so tightly its horn pierced the skin on his palm.

Scenting blood, the wolves bayed and prowled closer.

"GET AWAY!" he shouted. He screamed at the top of his lungs and waved his arms wildly, hoping the noise would scare the wolves away.

The wolves backed away, but the werewolf stood his ground.

There was a clap of thunder.

Suddenly Petros knew what he had to do. He clutched the unicorn charm tighter and shouted up into the sky.

"HELP ME, STORM CHASERS!"

A bolt of lightning hit the ground, followed by a deep rumble of thunder. Petros gasped as a storm-grey unicorn stepped out of the branching crater the lightning had scorched in the grass.

The unicorn swished his bright yellow tail and the air crackled with electricity. The wolves' fur stood on end and they backed away nervously. The vicious werewolf snarled and swiped at the unicorn with his claws. Lowering his head, the Storm Chaser shot a bolt of lightning out of his star-bright horn, striking the werewolf and knocking him over.

The unicorn reared up and slammed its hooves into the ground. There was a mighty boom of thunder and rain began to fall.

Through the heavy downpour, Petros could see the wolves slinking away, tails between their legs. The werewolf lay on the ground, motionless.

"Thank you," said Petros. He reached out to stroke the unicorn's yellow mane and felt the faint crackle of static electricity. The Storm Chaser nodded, then galloped away through the rain. There was another loud rumble of thunder as his hooves pounded up the mountainside.

So the legend is true! thought Petros, as thunder rolled out across the land.

Lifting the trembling lamb into his arms, Petros ran through the rain to the cave's shelter. The sheep bleated happily at their return.

The storm raged all through the night, but by the morning the sun was shining. As Petros and his flock headed home they came across the strange man, lying on the ground. The wild look had gone from his eyes, his wolfish leer replaced with a dazed look of relief.

"The curse," he gasped. "It is finally broken. A werewolf bit me months ago as I tended my flock on this mountainside. Ever since I have felt like a different person ... but the unicorn saved me!"

When Petros returned home, his mother was just as overjoyed to see him as Delphi's had been. She threw her arms around her son. "I thought a werewolf had got you," she sobbed.

"Nearly," said Petros. "But a Storm Chaser saved us." He took out the unicorn carving and showed it to his parents. From that day forward, Petros never went up the mountain without his lucky charm. And never again did werewolves trouble the villagers or their flocks during the full moon.

Winged Lion

Winged lions are proud and majestic creatures. In some mythologies they fly through the sky, bringing light to the world.

Powerful wings
for swift flight

Golden mane
made of light

MYTH FILE EIGHT:

Dawn Roar

Winged lions appear in a number of
different mythologies and cultures.
They are proud and fierce creatures.

The winged lion in this story has an especially
important power. With its golden, light-giving
mane, it soars through the sky, bringing light
to an enchanted world. But it needs help from
a young girl and a Dawn Spirit, a magnificent
unicorn that can grant wishes.

Secret *of the* Dawn

Aurora pushed open the door of her grandmother's
study. She had only passed away a few weeks
ago and Aurora still missed everything about
her - the laugh that made her whole body shake,
her big hugs - but most of all, her stories.

Grandma was a writer, and the shelves of her study were lined with books about wicked sorcerers, gods, goddesses and mythical creatures.

Aurora ran her finger along a shelf and came to a book she'd never seen before: *The Magical Unicorn Society Handbook*. She took it down and leafed through the pages, which were filled with beautiful illustrations of unicorns. Sitting down on the window seat, she read it from cover to cover.

When she turned the final page, an envelope with her name on it fell out. Curious, Aurora tore it open. Inside there was a slim golden key and a handwritten note on a piece of paper. It read:

Dear Aurora,

I hope you will become our newest member.

Love always,

Grandma

At the bottom of the page, her grandmother's name was printed, along with a mysterious title - Head of Literature and Lore, The Magical Unicorn Society.

How odd, Aurora thought. She turned the key over in her hand. *I wonder what it opens ...*

Aurora ran around the house, trying the key in every door she could find, but it didn't fit in any of the locks.

"What are you up to?" asked her mother, who was packing up Grandma's pots and pans in the kitchen.

"Um ... nothing," said Aurora, innocently. She felt certain Grandma would want the key and the letter to be a secret.

Aurora went outside to see if there was anything in the garden that the key might fit. It was still early, and the grass was wet with dew. She tried the key in the shed, but had no luck. But just then, Samba, her grandmother's ginger cat, jumped down from an ivy-covered wall at the end of the yard and gave a loud meow. Glancing over, Aurora saw a door hidden behind the ivy leaves.

"How have I never seen that before?" she wondered.

Aurora took the golden key and tried it in the lock. It was a perfect fit!

Opening the creaky door, Aurora stepped inside and found herself in a corner of the garden she'd never been before. And standing there, under a bower of roses, was an amazing blue unicorn. It had a sparkling yellow horn, the colour of sunshine, and its tail and mane shimmered with the pinks and purples of the morning sky. It looked exactly like one of the illustrations in Grandma's unicorn book.

"Are you a Dawn Spirit?" Aurora asked.

The unicorn scuffed the ground.

Aurora stared at the beautiful creature in amazement. It was as if she'd stepped right into one of her grandma's stories. She knew from the book she'd read that Dawn Spirit's could grant wishes. She closed her eyes and made a silent plea …

The unicorn lowered its head. Aurora understood that it was inviting her to get on. Heart racing, she climbed onto the unicorn's back. She gripped the silky mane and gasped as the unicorn leaped up and soared through the air.

Wind rushed against Aurora's face as the Dawn Spirit flew higher and higher into the sky. The house was now just a tiny speck, far below them, and soon they reached the clouds.

Aurora couldn't see more than a few inches in front of her, but she could hear something - a wailing noise travelling on the air. The unicorn burst out above the clouds and came to a halt right on top of them.

"Hello?" Aurora called out.

Ahead of her, an ethereal woman walking on the clouds came forward. She was wearing a white gown and had a golden tiara perched on her head. When she got closer, Aurora could see that her beautiful face was full of woe.

"What's wrong?" Aurora asked her. "Who are you?"

"I am Thea," said the woman, "the goddess of light in the cloud kingdom. But my light has disappeared. My magical winged lion, Leo, has been captured by Erebus, the god of darkness. Winged lions bring light to the world. Without him, we'll be bathed in darkness forever."

"Why would Erebus do such a thing?" asked Aurora.

"Our powers normally balance each other out," she continued. "But by taking Leo, he would be able to take control of the land. And I would be powerless to stop him."

Aurora slid off the Dawn Spirit's back and stood on the clouds. "Maybe we can help," she offered.

"I would be eternally grateful," said Thea. "Erebus resides in a labyrinth made of magic. You will find Leo imprisoned at its centre."

The goddess led them through the darkening clouds to the entrance of the labyrinth. "Good luck, and beware Erebus's dark magic," she told them.

Aurora and the Dawn Spirit stepped inside the labyrinth. They turned left and wandered through the narrow, twisting passages. The walls were covered in thorny plants which scratched at them, as if trying to keep them out. Topiary beasts and monsters, sculpted from the prickly shrubbery, leered down through the darkness. Every time Aurora looked up at them, they had shifted position. Some even seemed to change shape, with one turning from an enormous bull to a three-headed dog and back again.

Go back ... the rustling branches whispered in the dark.

Aurora fought the urge to turn and run away. Guided by instinct alone, she and the Dawn Spirit pressed ahead, until finally they reached the centre of the maze.

In the dim light, Aurora saw a powerful figure in a black cloak. He wore a horned helmet and held a spear made of a dark metal. Next to him was a magnificent winged lion trapped behind the bars of a golden cage.

"You made it to the centre. I am impressed," said Erebus. "But only magic stronger than my own can unlock the cage."

Aurora's heart sank. She had no magic - she was just an ordinary girl.

At that moment, the Dawn Spirit nudged Aurora's pocket with her nose. Aurora stuck her hand inside and took out the gold key her grandmother had left her. It glinted in the faint light from the unicorn's horn.

"Not so fast," cautioned Erebus, holding up his spear. "You may have a key, but there are three locks, and only one of them unlocks it. If you choose the wrong one, the winged lion will be trapped forever."

Aurora looked on, nervously. The three locks looked exactly the same. Even though she might get it wrong, Aurora knew she needed to try. She had promised to help Thea.

Suddenly, a memory flooded into her head, as clear as daylight. She was a little girl, curled up on her grandmother's lap. Grandma was telling her a story about three ancient gods who had carved up the world into three kingdoms - the sky, the sea and the underworld.

The underworld, Aurora thought. *The third and darkest kingdom. Surely Erebus, god of darkness, would pick the third lock.*

She bent down to the third lock, inserted and turned the key, and the door to the cage opened. Immediately, Leo the winged lion bounded out of the cage.

"Noooo!" howled Erebus. He aimed his spear at Aurora and the unicorn, but the Dawn Spirit was too fast for him.

The enormous lion opened his mighty jaws, spread his wings and let out a ferocious roar. Springing forward, he charged at Erebus, pushing him backwards into the cage.

Quickly, Aurora dashed forward and closed the door tight, trapping the god of darkness inside. With Erebus trapped, the balance of the cloud kingdom would be restored.

With another roar, the lion leapt into the air. His golden fur blazed as brightly as the sun as he moved, restoring light across the sky.

Aurora and the Dawn Spirit made their way out of the
maze. It no longer looked threatening. The ominous, thorny
walls had turned into beautiful rose bushes, blooming with
fragrant pink and red flowers. When they emerged from the
maze, Thea was waiting for them with Leo by her side. The
winged lion purred as the dazzling goddess stroked his fur.

"Thank you so much for saving Leo," said Thea, "and
restoring the light."

"I still don't understand how I did it," said Aurora. "Erebus
said only something more powerful than his magic could
break the spell. But I'm not powerful at all."

"My child, the one thing stronger than magic is the bond
between you and the ones you love," said Thea, taking
Aurora's hand and giving it a squeeze.

Aurora thought of the gold key in her pocket - a gift from
her grandmother.

Aurora said goodbye and climbed onto the Dawn Spirit's
back. Together, they returned to the secret walled garden

behind her grandmother's house.

"Thank you for granting my wish and taking me on an incredible journey," said Aurora, stroking the unicorn's mane.

She had wished she could be with her grandmother again, listening to one of her stories, but instead, the Dawn Spirit had given Aurora something truly special - an amazing adventure story of her own.

Leaving the garden, Aurora locked the door behind her and slipped the golden key into her pocket. Samba the cat was waiting for her on the grass, like a miniature version of Leo. Smiling to herself, Aurora hurried into the house to write down the story of the adventure she'd just had. Her grandmother was gone, but Aurora couldn't wait to carry on her work telling incredible stories as the newest member of the Magical Unicorn Society.

WHICH MYTHICAL CREATURE ARE YOU?

Everyone has a distinct personality, and we're all drawn to different types of mythical creature. Find out which creature you are drawn to and what that says about your personality on the following page.

Good: it's always better to help people.

The ability to fly.

Is it better to use this power for good or for mischief?

Mischief: superpowers should be about having fun.

START
What type of superpower would you prefer?

Money and power: it's good to have nice things.

Super strength.

What's more important: money and power or animals and nature?

Animals and nature: living things are beautiful.

Would you prefer to fly at dawn or during the night?

Dawn: it's the most beautiful time of the day.

WINGED LION

Night: it's nice to see the stars shine and the Moon's glow.

PHOENIX

Would you prefer to live on top of a mountain or in a secluded woodland?

Mountain: the views would be amazing.

SAND DRAGON

Woodland: it's special to be close to nature.

FOREST SPRITES AND IMPS

Are you quiet and cautious or loud and powerful?

Quiet: it's better to not draw too much attention to yourself.

APEP THE SERPENT

Loud: you have to let everyone know you're there.

STONE TROLL

Would you prefer to live in the sea or on the land?

Land: the trees, hills, meadows and valleys are the best.

WEREWOLF

Sea: the fish, sharks, coral reefs and lagoons are really cool.

KRAKEN

MYTHICAL CREATURES EXPLAINED

Find out what your mythical creature represents.

WINGED LION

Winged Lions represent those full of optimism and joy, with bright and sunny personalities.

PHOENIX

Those represented by phoenixes love freedom. They also have a mystical side and an affinity with the Moon.

SAND DRAGON

Those represented by Sand Dragons value independence and freedom, and have a wandering spirit.

FOREST SPRITES AND IMPS

Forest sprites and imps represent those with cheeky personalities, and those that love to have fun and play games.

APEP THE SERPENT

Apep represents those with
strong personalities, who like
to lead and be in charge.

STONE TROLL

Stone trolls represent those
with inner strength, who have
strong opinions and wants.

WEREWOLF

Werewolves represent those with
many sides to their personalities,
and those who love the outdoors.

KRAKEN

Those represented by the Kraken
have hidden depths. They also
prefer their own company.

These are just eight of the amazing mythical creatures that exist, or have
existed, in our world. The Department of Unicorns, Myths and Monsters is
always on the lookout for more. For more information and to join the M.U.S.,
visit www.magicalunicornsociety.co.uk. And stay alert: you never know
when a unicorn, or another mythical creature, might cross your path.